For Rachel, who told me,
and Bruce, who told her
D.N.

For Matthew
E.F.

Scholastic Children's Books,
Commonwealth House, 1-19 New Oxford Street,
London WC1A 1NU, UK
a division of Scholastic Ltd

London • New York • Toronto • Sydney • Auckland
Mexico City • New Delhi • Hong Kong

First published in New Zealand by Ashton Scholastic, 1994.
First published in the UK by Scholastic Ltd, 1995.
This edition published by Little Hippo, an imprint of Scholastic Ltd, 2000.

Text copyright © Diana Noonan, 1994
Illustrations copyright © Elizabeth Fuller, 1994

ISBN 0 439 01461 1

Printed in Italy by Amadeus S.p.A. - Rome

All rights reserved

2 4 6 8 10 9 7 5 3 1

The rights of Diana Noonan and Elizabeth Fuller to be identified as the
author and illustrator of this work respectively have been asserted by them
in accordance with the Copyright, Designs and Patents Act, 1988.

The Best-Loved Bear

The Best-Loved Bear

Diana Noonan Elizabeth Fuller

Little Hippo

It was almost holiday time.

"Let's do something special," said Mr McDonald.

"Let's have a best-loved bear competition."

Tim was worried.
He had a bear called Toby
and he loved him very much.
But that was the problem.

Tim loved Toby so much
that he'd hugged off almost all his fur.

Tim loved Toby so much
that he'd sucked a piece of
his left ear right off,
and worn a hole in his nose with kisses.

Tim loved Toby so much
that he even shared his ice creams with him
and now Toby was all sticky.

Toby could never win a bear competition
no matter how hard Tim tried to make him
look new again.
And he did try.

He tried to brush
the little bit of fur
that was left on Toby.

and he washed off as much of the ice cream
as he could.

Toby could never win a bear competition
no matter how hard Tim tried to make him
look new again.
And he did try.

He tried to brush
the little bit of fur
that was left on Toby.

He tried to mend Toby's left ear with a bandage.

He put a sticking plaster on Toby's nose,

and he washed off as much of the ice cream
as he could.

The next day,
Tim carried Toby to school
in a brown paper bag
so that no one could see
how tatty he looked.

"Put your bears on the table," said Mr McDonald.
"Mrs Hall is going to be the judge.
Hurry up, Tim. Where's your bear?"

Tim took Toby out of the bag.

Mrs Hall, the head teacher, looked at number one.
"This is a smart bear," she said.
"Someone has made this bear a new jacket.
He must be loved."

Then she looked at number two.
"And this bear has a soft, well-brushed coat.
Someone must love this bear, too."

Then Mrs Hall looked at bear number three.
"Now this bear must be loved very much," she said.
"Someone has been shining his nose and paws."

Mrs Hall spent a long time looking at the bears.
"This is a hard competition to judge," she said.

Then she looked at number twenty.
"My word," she said,
"number twenty is an interesting bear."

Tim went red.

"Look at his left ear," said Mrs Hall.
"Someone has tried to mend it with a bandage.
And his nose has a sticking plaster on it.
Perhaps it was worn out with kisses.
This bear has had the fur hugged off him," she said,
"and someone has been feeding him ice cream."

"This bear has been loved to bits!"
said Mrs Hall with a big smile.
"I am going to give the gold medal
for the best-loved bear to number twenty!"

Tim couldn't stop grinning.
He tied the medal around Toby's neck . . .

and that afternoon
he carried him
on his shoulders
all the way home.